MYSTERY AT POINT BEACH

BEACH

~ Book 5 ~

The Ringmaster

Kate Jungwirth

Deborah Erdmann

of
Worlds Only Circus School
INDOOR CIRCUS
1939

It is the stars, the superstitious will tell you, that foretell the day of our birth, the profession and characteristics which will haunt us all the days of our life. If this be true, the stars must have swung with vigor in their orbits on that October 1, 1880, when William G. Schultz was born. For before many years had passed, this brilliant young man was swinging too, and in short order was himself a brilliant star in the orbit traveled by the luminaries of the professional show world.

CHAPTER 1

"Dominic, you're missing out on the country view with your nose in your phone." Grandpa Bob pointed out the cattle on the hillside from his truck window. "Look at the herd of cows on your right. Do you see the black one with the white stripe around his belly?"

"Sorry, GB. I was just texting Forest to let him know we'll be at Point Beach soon." I reread my message to Forest.

Big news! GB is going to propose to Windsong. He bought a ring and everything. Can you believe it?

"Dominic, you didn't even look at the cow."

I stuck my nose to the window to make him happy. "I don't see it, Grandpa."

GB sighed. "You missed it. That's what they call an Oreo cow, but it's actually a Belted Galloway. They call it the 'Oreo' because it resembles the Oreo cookie. That's your favorite, isn't it?"

My phone dinged with Forest's reply: *No way! Does Windsong know?*

"Are you listening, Dominic? I said *Oreos!*"

I glanced over at GB. He looked annoyed.

"Oreos? Sure. Thanks, Grandpa."

"Hmphhff." GB shook his head.

I typed my reply to Forest. *I think he wants to surprise Windsong, so don't say anything.*

Windsong is Forest and Sailor's grandma. The three of them camp with us at Point Beach every summer. That's how we all met and became close friends. Forest, Sailor, and I even solved a few mysteries at the campground.

I was so busy texting that I hadn't noticed we'd arrived at Point Beach. GB slowly angled the Nimrod, his relic, stone-age camper, up to the park office.

"Well, lookie here!" GB pointed to a large, colorful poster taped in the window. "The circus is coming to town!"

I leaned past GB to see the poster. The title "BIG TOP CIRCUS" was displayed in large letters above a clown with fuzzy red hair, a big red nose, and a wide mouth circled in bright red lipstick.

"Well, if it isn't my favorite detectives!" Ranger Sally greeted us with a smile as we drove up to the office. It looked like she had put on a little more weight. She was tightly wedged into the window.

"Hello, Sally." GB nodded and winked. "Actually, my grandson Dominic is the sleuth. I'm just the old geezer who tags along."

"Say," she leaned forward, "did you boys see that a big tent circus will be here this weekend? Ranger Rick will have his hands full, to be sure." She blushed at the mention of his name.

Ugh. Another romance at Point Beach. Sally appeared head-over-heels for the ranger. My breakfast almost came back up.

"No doubt the ranger's on top of things." GB grimaced as he reached for the reservation ticket and pulled ahead.

As we ambled down the winding road to our campsite, I finished my conversation with Forest. *Al-*

most there. We'll stop in after Nimrod is resurrected from the dead.

GB and I had the whole setup routine down to a science. In a matter of minutes, the camper roof was raised, the door and windows fastened, and the safety supports set in place. Once the shell went up, we headed inside, where a pungent mildew odor greeted us. It made my eyes water.

"Race you at making our beds!" I shouted to GB.

I specialized at making a bed—army style. After tugging the sheet so tight you could flip a dime on it, I flung my red-and-black-checkered quilt over the top before reaching into the cooler for an Orange Crush.

What can I say? You gotta have routines, otherwise the world is absolute chaos.

I sat down on my cot, feeling smug over my win. "When are you gonna pop the question?"

"Wipe that orange mustache off your face, Dom." GB's eyes flashed beneath his bushy eyebrows. "I'll ask when the time is right. That's when."

I wiped my mouth with the back of my hand.

"That doesn't sound like much of a plan, Grandpa."

GB reached into his flannel shirt pocket, pulling out a small black box. "See here? I already bought the ring."

He opened the box, revealing a shiny silver band with a small diamond set between two engraved hearts.

"There's a candlelight walk on Ridges Trail tonight," he continued. "Friends of Point Beach posted it on their Facebook page. I figured it would be a perfect opportunity. And if there's a full moon, all the better."

He glanced at me. "I hope it goes without saying, this is a secret. I want Windsong to be surprised."

Uggh … too late.

"Um, would it be okay to let Forest and Sailor in on it if they promise not to tell?"

"I suppose so, as long as they keep it a secret." He put the box into the drawer next to his bed. "Help me unpack the snacks your mom made, and then we can go meet the others."

I have to admit, I was excited that Windsong's

hippie friends were back at the campground for their annual reunion. The last time they were here, Forest, Sailor and I were in over our heads trying to solve our first mystery at Point Beach.

It was comforting to have the help of a few old-timers who have been around the block a few times, even if they did have dreadlocks, tattoos and tie-dye shirts.

Since it was just a short trek to the group site, we decided to take our bikes. Over the years, Point Beach had become my home-away-from-home. I knew every trail and tree by heart.

We had just crossed the road when we saw something unusual looming in the distance.

"What in tarnation ...?" GB stopped short, which resulted in me doing a somersault over my handlebars.

Dazed, I looked in the direction that had captured his attention. Nestled in the woods behind a row of canvas tents stood a small but majestic, burgundy-striped circus tent. A string of light bulbs dotted the tent poles. But I think it was the monkey hanging from the lights that had GB dumbfounded.

"Is this the circus we saw the flyer for?" I slowly stood to my feet, rubbing the back of my head where a goose egg was sure to appear thanks to that tumble.

"Hi, boys!" Windsong emerged from her lime-green trailer. The door slammed behind her, which scared off the monkey, who made a mad dash for the woods. "Jughead, get back here!" she yelled after it before turning her attention back to us. "Aren't you a sight for sore eyes!"

Talk about a "sight." She was dressed in her usual Bohemian attire, but something was different. She had dyed her white braids hot-pink.

"Good to see you, Windsong." GB furtively glanced up at her head.

"Oh, Bobby, my pink hair must be a shock. When I signed up to sell cotton candy at the circus, a friend suggested I have some fun with it." She twirled full circle, her flowered chiffon skirt swishing around her bare feet. "Is this festive, or what?"

GB grinned. "It's not every day a person sees a

circus in the woods."

I don't think he meant the tent. Or the monkey.

He took in the view around the campsite. "Looks like there's a whole theme going on here."

What's the theme? Humiliation?

"This tent belongs to my friend, Archie. He's the circus ringmaster and likes to do his makeup private- ly." She winked at me. "And the squirrel monkey? That would be Jughead. He belongs to Archie."

"Archie?" GB scratched his head.

"You haven't met Archie, yet. It was his idea to color my hair. He's been working at the Big Apple Cir- cus in New York the past few summers."

"Where did the monkey go?" I thought I saw a flash of fur in the woods.

Before Windsong could answer, a middle-aged man with wild red curls and black-rimmed glasses came walking out of the tent.

"Archie Valentine, come and meet my good friends, Bobby and Dominic Dorsey!" Windsong waved her hand in our direction. "They're famous in this neck of the woods."

"Famous, you say?" As he spoke, I couldn't help but notice the crooked teeth behind his thin, red lips. I had goosebumps.

He looked downright creepy.

CHAPTER 2

"Dominic, Forest and Sailor have a reputation for soloving a few mysteries here at Point Beach." Windsong shook her finger at Archie. "You've missed a lot these past few summers."

"Well, I guess I have. Taking in teens and preparing them for the circus keeps me busy."

Archie leaned in for a closer look at me. His Coke-bottle eyeglasses made his pupils look enormous. "How old are you, young man?"

"I just turned fourteen, Sir."

"Look me up in two more years. You'd make an excellent candidate for the youth circus."

Was that supposed to be a compliment? I shrunk back, suddenly feeling analyzed under the scrutiny of his magnifying glasses.

GB extended his hand to Archie. "Nice to meet you." He shook Archie's hand, nodding in approval at the baggy pants and striped tie he sported. "It's been a while since I attended a circus show."

Archie turned, scanning the woods behind the tent. "It won't be much of a show without Jug."

"Don't worry, Archie. We'll find Jughead," Windsong said.

GB chuckled. "Sorry, but the names 'Archie' and 'Jughead' remind me of the comic strip *The Archies*. Dominic's too young to remember, but his mother was practically raised on their hit song, 'Sugar, Sugar.'"

Ugh … I could feel some "hot pink" of my own, coloring my cheeks. GB sure knew how to embarrass a guy. Time to change the subject.

"So, Windsong, where is everybody? I texted Forest that we'd be here soon."

"The circus is setting up in the field next to the playground." She pointed in the direction of the lake. "The kids and the others are over there right now. Everyone who helps set up gets free popcorn and soda pop. Why don't you fellas head over there? I'll help Archie find Jughead, and then we'll join you."

A steady clanking reverberated through the trees as we approached the park.

At the center of the grounds, a few strong men used sledgehammers to pound in stakes that held up a large red-and-white-striped circus tent with poles. Others bustled about, tightening ropes and carrying equipment.

We leaned our bikes against a nearby tree. GB walked over to where some of Windsong's hippie friends were putting up fencing.

I made a beeline toward the animal trailers where a bunch of teenagers were carrying feed and buckets of water.

"Hey, you over there ... why don't you 'step right up' and give us a hand?" a voice called from a flatbed parked near the Big Top's entrance.

I recognized it immediately. Bleach-blonde Forest was balancing a platform in his arms with Sailor fumbling to hold up the other end.

"Dominic!" She dropped her side and skipped over to embrace me in a hug. "Thank goodness. You're just in time."

"What—for the clown show?" I laughed as I helped lift the platform back up. "You're lucky I've been working out."

Forest eyed my biceps and smirked. "No comment."

Inside the tent the construction was well underway. A tightrope stretched across with a net below. Towers of lights surrounded the center stage; props placed along the sides.

"That goes over here." A girl about my age with a British accent motioned to us.

"Hello, mates. I'm Emily," she said after we secured the platform. Her blue eyes glistened in the fluorescent lights that hung from the tent roof.

"I'm Sailor, this is my brother, Forest, and our

friend, Dominic. The three of us are practically related."

"Related?" I raised my hands. "Grandpa Bob was
a little thrown off by your grandma's neon hairdo and
the clown who was looking for his lost monkey."

"That's my uncle," Emily told us.

I laughed. "The monkey's your uncle?"

"She's talking about the clown, not the monkey,"
Forest interrupted.

"Quite right," Emily said. "Though he's actually
not *my* uncle. We all call Archie 'Uncle Jolly.' That's his
stage name."

"You're not from around here, then?" Her accent
intrigued me.

"I'm from England. Uncle Jolly offered me a circus gig in New York, so I came here to join him. I love
all the animals, and the experience will help me pre-
pare for larger venues in the future. Uncle Jolly said I
may even take over his job as ringmaster someday."

Out of the corner of my eye, I caught sight of a
small furball with a long tail, a white face, and black

muzzle slipping beneath the tent flap.

He paused to look around for a moment before scrambling toward a familiar blue-haired elderly lady who had a banana sticking out of her purse.

"Look!" I pointed. "The monkey came back and just stole Sadie's banana."

Sadie Buckley and her husband, Bert, were the camp hosts at Point Beach since forever.

"Oh, dear. Jughead is a bit cheeky, you know." Emily waved to a worker carrying in a unicycle behind us. "Well, the show must go on, and I'd best scoot off now. Cheerio!"

"Sayonara." Sailor waved.

"She's British, not Japanese." Forest rolled his eyes.

Sailor ignored him and turned toward the little thief and his latest victim. "Hey, Mrs. Buckley. I hope you didn't plan on eating that banana."

"What?" Sadie peered down at the leftover peel. "I see our three great detectives are already spotting crimes." She patted the monkey on the head. "It's okay, little Bughead. I have more where that came from."

"It's 'Jughead,'" I moaned.

Mrs. Buckley was famous for getting names wrong.

Not knowing the first thing about detaining a monkey, I was relieved to see Archie walk in with Windsong in tow. Giving a whistle, he bent down on one knee as Jughead scampered over.

Sadie approached Archie. "Mr. Valentine, I presume?"

"As far as you know," Archie snickered.

The sarcasm seemed to go over her head. God love 'er.

"That certainly is a well-trained monkey you have there." Sadie nodded.

"Thanks. He catches on really quick. I'm even teaching him to ride a unicycle." Archie clipped a leash to Jug's gold-studded collar. "Hard to believe I ordered him from a vintage comic book ad."

"For real?" I didn't know if I could take this clown seriously.

"Nah, I'm pulling your leg," Archie chuckled. "Jughead was found orphaned on an island when we adopted him. Although, back in the 60s, you really could order strange things from comic books, like sea-monkeys, jumping beans, and x-ray glasses."

Sailor's eyes widened. "That's crazy!"

On cue, Bert Buckley drove his golf cart into the tent with GB riding shotgun.

"Watch out!" GB yelled as Bert nearly crashed into the center pole holding up the entire tent.

"Saints preserve us!" Sadie nearly leaped out of her thick-soled orthopedic shoes.

Bert stopped short of the tent pole, slamming on the brakes. Gears grinding, he shifted the cart in reverse and made his way over.

"Your chariot awaits," he called to Sadie.

"Maybe someone else should be doing the driving?" Archie's voice strained.

"Mr. Buckley's hard of hearing. You have to yell, otherwise he can't hear you," I said.

"Actually," Sadie said, "Bert got new hearing aids. He can hear just fine. He just can't drive."

"Next year, I'll get my license." Forest leaned

toward me. "It'll be a challenge, all these old guys with hearing aids and magnified eyeglasses driving around."

"Whew, that was a close one." GB mopped his forehead as he hobbled out the passenger side so Sadie could get in. Once they exited the tent and the coast was clear, we circled the arena, taking in all the curiosities.

"This is quite the operation." GB looked around the tent like a kid in a candy store.

"Few realize how much work goes into putting on a circus. It doesn't just go up 'poof,' like an umbrella." Archie popped open his fingers on both hands.

"We met one of your students," I said to Archie. "Are all the performers going to be kids our age?"

"You'd better believe it," he replied. "They practice all year, and travel to shows during the summer. Windsong's invitation to Point Beach for the reunion was perfect timing. We just had a cancelation at the Circus Museum in Baraboo."

He leaned in, his red-stained grin widening,

"Say, did you know there was a man named Billy Schultz from Manitowoc who toured with the Ringling Bros. Circus?

"He started out in a clown acrobatic comedy act, then came back here to open a youth training school. It eventually became a big deal and even made history as one of the first of its kind. Circus recruiters came from all over the countryside to scope out new prospects."

"There was a time when I thought I was going to run away and join the circus." Windsong's eyes misted. "Remember that, Archie? You tried to talk me into becoming a trapeze artist." She chuckled.

"How could I forget! You would've been a show-stopper." Archie ran his arm across her shoulders, pulling her close.

It appears the training school wasn't the only thing with "history." Windsong and Archie were really hitting it off.

I glanced at GB. The expression on his face looked forced, like a marionette with a painted smile.

This could be trouble.

CHAPTER 3

After that humiliating display, it was all I could do to keep GB from pouting.

That evening, he had settled into his hammock for a nap, his snores synchronized to the loud brass playing from his AM/FM radio—classic tunes by Romy Gosz, a star performer in the Wisconsin Polka Hall of Fame.

"I wonder what Windsong sees in that clown friend of hers." I sat with Forest and Sailor at our picnic table on site #127.

"Your grandpa sure has some pretty 'big shoes' to fill." Forest laughed.

"Quit clowning around." I slapped at a pesky mosquito. "I'm being serious."

"Maybe we should show GB the ropes—you know, make him more romantic." Sailor squinted at a thread of clouds floating above the pine trees.

Just then, GB moseyed out of the hammock and took a seat in his lounge chair, where he proceeded to clean his teeth with a toothpick.

Time to take action.

"Grandpa, if you're going to get married, you're going to have to stop acting the way you do," I said.

"What way?" He removed the toothpick.

"The way you act … you have to become different," Sailor suggested.

"I don't understand."

"You know, the way you always are?" Forest asked.

"Yeah …?" GB raised an eyebrow.

"Don't be that way," Forest shot back.

"We're telling you this for your own good." Sailor put her hands on her hips. "There's some major competition in case you haven't noticed. You need to step up your game."

"For your information," GB retorted, "I was married to Dominic's grandmother for forty years. I have plenty of prior experience up my sleeve."

"That's not the only thing on your sleeve." I pointed to a large ketchup stain from the evening dinner of campfire potatoes and steak kabobs.

"I guess I'd better go change. The sun's going down and Windsong will be here any minute." He checked his watch as he hurried inside Nimrod.

It was out of our hands. Whether or not GB could make the love connection was all up to him. We were just about to start a game of beanbag toss when the sound of rattling drawers caught my attention.

"Dominic, did you take the ring? It's not in the drawer where I put it," GB called through the screen.

"Are you sure it's not there?"

GB sighed in exasperation. "I'm looking into an empty drawer. Do you see a ring in here?"

I ran inside with Forest and Sailor right on my heels. He was right. No black box. Together, we rifled through every drawer in the camper, but the ring wasn't anywhere to be found.

GB pulled on his goatee, a nervous habit of his. "This is a heck of a time for the ring to go missing. Tonight's the candlelight walk."

"I saw you put it in the drawer." I shook my head. "What are you going to do now?"

"What else can I do but go ahead with my plans? I already asked Windsong out for an evening stroll, and she's excited about it."

"Maybe it will still turn up in time. We'll leave you to finish getting ready, Grandpa."

As I took a step down from the camper, something gave way under my foot, and I fell forward. Catching my balance, I looked down.

"Funny—I wonder where *that* came from?" I picked up a yellow peel off the ground and tossed it into the fire pit.

Then a realization hit me.

"A banana peel?" I turned to Forest and Sailor.

"Guys, are you thinking what I'm thinking?"

"You and Grandpa Bob are slobs?" Sailor took a wild guess.

"What? GB's a neat freak. No, I was thinking that maybe Jughead was being 'a bit cheeky' again."

As I sped through the campground on my Trek, Forest and Sailor had a hard time keeping up. I noticed a spiral of smoke coming from the group campsite. The hippies were back from helping the circus kids.

"Hey, high five, dude! Gimme some skin." Jim walked over from the fire pit. I met Jim a few years ago. In fact, he was a prime suspect in Ranger Rick's investigation of the Sundae Wars, thanks to his lactose intolerance tendencies.

"Hi, Jim!" I reached up to high five him back, which was part of Jim's own special secret hand-shake—we proceeded to fist bump, turn in a circle, pinch our noses, and slap each other alongside the head.

Having satisfied the greeting, we headed to the fire pit where we found the usual assortment of hip-

pies. A few ladies with headbands and beads, a bearded guy with dreadlocks playing a harmonica, and Jim,
dressed in the usual attire—bell bottoms and a paisley
shirt.

"We're looking for Archie. Have you seen him?"
I looked all around for his crazy red hairdo.

"Not lately. He's been hangin' with Windsong all
day," Jim said.

That concerned me. "Are they … dating or something?" I shuffled my feet.

The hippies all looked at each other. Rupert, the
bearded man with dreadlocks, leaned forward. "I
know your grandpa is fond of Windsong. But you
should know that she and Archie go way back."

I took an empty seat in the circle of chairs. "This
isn't good. I'm not supposed to tell anyone, but GB was
planning on proposing to Windsong. He even bought a
ring, only it was stolen from our camper."

"We suspect Archie's monkey took it," Forest
added.

"Dude, that's a bummer!" Jim said. "Come to

think of it, we were just talking about how quite a few of our things have gone missing lately."

"Yeah, man, something funny is going on here." Rupert rubbed his chin hairs.

Harmony, the woman sitting next to him wearing a tie-dyed tank top turned to me. "Hey, honey, no need to be so mellow. Your grandpa can give her my mood ring!"

She set down her Big Gulp mug, slipped the gaudy ring off her finger, and handed it to me.

"That's one heck of a ring!" I eyed the oversized greenish-yellow stone that was turning grayish-brown in my palm. "I know GB would rather have the diamond one he bought, but I can ask if he'd like to borrow it."

Jim reached for his guitar—our cue to leave. Besides, there was no use waiting around. Without more evidence, all we had to go on was just a hunch.

I pulled Forest and Sailor aside. "I'll drop this off for GB and meet you at Ridges Trail. I wonder how he's going to pull this off with a mood ring."

Just before sunset, the sky surrendered its color, giving way to a light shade of gray. Flickering candles scattered along the trail cast illumination into the dark forest.

"This looks like as good a spot as any," I whispered to Forest and Sailor. We crouched down behind a row of bushes.

"I'm sick to my stomach about the missing ring," Sailor said. "I hope GB goes through with it."

"He's got the mood ring," I interrupted. "I'm sure he'll give it a shot."

"If not, then there's no point to this stakeout," Forest complained. "Who wants to watch an elderly couple taking a walk in the woods? I'd rather sit through an Andy Griffith rerun on Netflix."

Sailor elbowed Forest. "What's wrong with you?

Dominic's grandpa is about to propose to our grand-ma. Don't you want to see it happen?"

Forest pretended to gag. "Not really."

"Shhh, I hear someone coming." I reached for my binoculars from my backpack.

On the other side of Ridges Trail, a figure in a clown costume clumsily made his way to a grouping of tall pines, ducking behind them. A bulbous red nose and an oversized shoe stuck out alongside a tree.

"Well, well. What do we have here?" I handed the binoculars to Forest.

While he surveyed the scene, I heard a rustling sound from the trail, accompanied by a shrill giggle.

CHAPTER 4

I grabbed the binoculars back from Forest. It was Ranger Sally in a yellow sundress, clutching Ranger Rick's hand.

I almost didn't recognize him out of uniform. The jean shorts didn't do any favors for his chicken legs, and without his Smokey the Bear hat, his slicked back hairstyle from the 50s had nowhere to hide.

Looks like this candlelight walk was stirring up all kinds of foolish ideas. It reminded me of a show GB watches all the time—*Fantasy Island.*

Just then, I spotted activity off to the right. The clown who had been crouched along the sidelines took one look at the ranger and headed for the hills, nearly tripping over his floppy shoes.

Interesting.

Ranger Rick bragged about his policing escapades as he walked out of sight with Ranger Sally.

I was about to relay what I had just seen to Forest and Sailor, when we spotted GB and Windsong on the trail in front of us. I issued a brisk "Shhh" warning.

Before I knew it, GB was down on one knee, next to a flickering candle. It was happening!

"Ooh, this is so exciting!" Sailor clasped her hands.

"Pipe down, jack-in-the-box," Forest hissed.

Oh, wait. GB was just tying his shoe.

I sighed. "False alarm."

Sailor giggled softly. I was smiling, myself. Poor GB. He wasn't very clever in the romance department.

"Hey! What are you turkeys doing down there?" Ranger Rick emerged from the shadowy ridge behind us.

"How did you get here so quickly from the trail?" I pointed to the path he'd just come from.

"I tracked your perfume."

"What perfume?" Forest frowned.

"Yer whatchacall, bug spray—Deep Woods Off, Black Flag, 409." He leaned in closer, his lip curling.

"Just what is it you're doing here in the bushes?"

"We're playing 'I Spy.' Would you like to join us?" Sailor asked.

"Maybe that's what you folks from *Illinois* do for fun, but in these parts, we know an even better game. It's called, 'Close your eyes, pick a number, and take a hike.'" He folded his arms. "Isn't it past your bedtime?"

"Ranger Rick … kids … what's going on here?" At that moment, Windsong and GB came walking into the clearing. Our cover was blown.

"You need to keep better track of your teenagers," Ranger Rick snarled. "I caught them back behind those bushes, spying on people."

GB chuckled. "Well, now, I wonder if they were hoping to catch some action on a romantic old fool."

"I've had it with you cheese heads! This is a violation of DNR code 23.095—damage to natural resources. Consider this a warning." Ranger Rick turned on his heel and stormed off, leaving us flabbergasted.

"What's his problem? We explained that we were

just playing a game," Forest said.

"Don't you get it? He thinks we were spying on him and Sally," I said. "He didn't know we were spying on GB and Windsong."

"Well, why on Earth would you be spying on us?" Windsong asked.

Ooooh, did I just say that out loud?

GB eyed the three of us. The romance had fizzled out like a sparkler.

"Well, kids, what do you say we roast some marshmallows? I'll get the fire started."

"Sounds good. We'll be right behind you," I said.

"What's the deal?" Forest asked when they were out of earshot.

"I'm curious as to what that clown was doing. Follow me." I led them across the trail and into a grove of pine trees.

When we got to the spot where the clown had been hiding, we discovered a brown paper bag leaning up against a tree.

Sailor peeked inside. "It's full of tomatoes!"

After a big breakfast of scrambled eggs and sausages, I sat back in my camp chair to let things settle.

Last night's tossing and turning from bad dreams required comfort food. GB's home cooking didn't disappoint, even if the missing ring hadn't turned up.

"Sorry we ruined your evening, Grandpa."

"You didn't ruin anything, Dominic. I got cold feet." GB stared into his black cup of coffee.

"Why didn't you use Harmony's ring?"

"I wasn't in the 'mood.'" He sighed. "I don't think I can propose to Windsong without a real ring. It's a tradition."

"It couldn't just disappear into thin air. What time did you notice the ring was missing, again?"

"I really didn't pay too much attention." He

paused. "It was around 7:34."

"Okay … and we got here around 2:00. So that leaves about a five and a half-hour window."

I was just starting in on the cinnamon rolls and orange juice when my cell phone started to buzz. It was a text from Forest. *Meet us on the beach.*

"Gotta run! We're looking into a few things, but I'll see you for lunch." I chugged the rest of my milk.

Following the beaten path behind our campsite, I hiked through the trees and over a grassy ridge down to the Lake Michigan shoreline. I found Forest and Sailor sitting on an uprooted tree trunk.

"So, any news?" I asked as we strolled along the beach toward the picnic area.

"Plenty," Forest replied. "We learned something that will shed a light on the mystery. Last night after we got back, Archie put on a magic show with one of the circus performers, Carla the illusionist."

"Yeah, everyone at our campsite was mesmerized," Sailor added. "After that they did a comedy skit with an orphan named Ginny and her parrot. Archie's training her to be some kind of fortune teller clown."

"Okay, and what does this have to do with Archie, Jughead, and the missing ring?"

"Just this," Sailor said, rubbing her hands together. "They used Jughead as part of their 'disappearing act.' Everything they set down, he picked up and hid. All they had to do was give him a banana."

"Disappearing act? Hmmm. So, the monkey is the missing link. I'm willing to bet on it," I exclaimed. "Remember that Jug was on the loose for a brief period while Nimrod was left unattended, plus the banana peel? It all adds up."

"But as for Archie, the only person here with a motive—turns out he has an alibi," Forest added. "He spent the entire day with Windsong, as we already know, and the rest of the night at the group camp, according to Jim."

"Then who was that clown we saw spying on GB and Windsong on Ridges Trail?" My mind was working overtime.

We stopped at a nearby picnic table. I took a few

minutes to appreciate the scenery. The waves gently rolled over the sand shore, and a few gulls soared overhead. Nature sure had a way of helping a person think.

"Here's another question." Forest broke the silence. "How did anyone know about the ring in the first place? It's been a secret."

"I only told you," I said to Forest.

"And the only person I told was Sailor," Forest responded.

We both looked at Sailor.

Her face contorted. "Well … I might've told one person while helping out at the circus grounds — a trick rider named May. Her horse, Zippy, had jeweled beads on her halter which reminded me of the ring."

"Well, if May can train a horse, maybe she trained Jug to rummage through old people's junk drawers for diamond rings?" I said, trying not to laugh. Then again, maybe it wasn't so far-fetched.

Sailor twisted her ponytail into a knot. "Don't get mad, but I may have mentioned it to a few others, too."

"Really great, Sailor." I held my head in my hands. "The entire circus crew probably knows about the ring by now. It could be anybody."

"I heard they're having a practice rehearsal today. Maybe we can find something out before the big show," Forest said. "At the very least, before they leave town."

We were just getting ready to head back when suddenly Jughead scampered toward us from the woods, jumped onto the picnic table, and right into my arms.

He was dressed in circus garb with a little hat askew on his head, his scrunched-up face tense, as if he was looking for help.

CHAPTER 5

Sadie and Bert Buckley followed right behind Jughead, with poor Sprinkles, their poodle, tangled in his leash alongside them. She was hopping in circles, trying to get to the monkey.

Sadie's cheeks flushed. "There you are, you little imp!"

Jug tried to squirm out of my grasp, but I held him tightly. "What seems to be the problem, Mrs. B?"

"Thank goodness we ran into you kids." She paused to catch her breath. "Bert and I had just returned back after our morning stroll with Sprinkles, when *Doug* came running out of our campsite. He had something shiny in his paw. Didn't he, Bert?"

"We just knew that monkey would be trouble. We knew." Bert yanked on the leash for the poodle to stay back. Sprinkles growled at Jughead.

"Bert immediately checked his fishing tackle box

which was on the picnic table. Wouldn'cha know, his vintage Musky Chippewa Minnow bait is missing. It's a collector's item!" Her eyes grew big as she relayed the event.

"Jughead!" I gave him a stern look. He actually looked remorseful. Either that, or he was one heck of an actor.

"Looks like we definitely have some monkey business going on," Forest joked.

"Yeah. It's obvious who took the ring, now." Sailor folded her arms.

"Well, there's only one way to find out." Forest eyed the monkey. "We need to find where Jug is keeping his stash. If the ring's there, we'll have our answer."

That gave me an idea. "Mrs. B, do you think that Sprinkles would be a good hunting dog?"

"I'm sure she's very good, Damien." She peered at us from behind thick glasses. "After all, she did track the chimp and lead us right to him."

"Um, it's Dominic." I reminded her even though

I knew it was no use. "We were wondering," I glanced at Forest and Sailor, "that is, if it's okay with you, if we could use Sprinkles to track down where Jughead's going with the stolen items?"

"What do you say, my wittle poopsie-woopsie?" Sadie bent down to ruffle Sprinkle's ears. "Should we give it a try?"

"Suit yourself. If that doesn't work, I have a mind to meet with Ranger Rick. He'll put a stop to this." Bert fished out his sunglasses from his flannel-shirt pocket. "I'm going back to the campsite to see if that rascal didn't drop my bait somewhere, and make sure nothing else was taken."

Sailor took the leash, holding tightly to Sprinkles while I dug in my pockets and pulled out a silver gum wrapper. Handing it to Jug, I set him on the ground to see what he would do. It worked like a charm. In a flash, he took the bait and scampered into the thicket.

"Let's go, Sprinky. Show us your stuff!" Sailor gave her some slack and Sprinkles took off, tugging on the leash, dragging Sailor behind as she went.

Keeping her nose to the ground, the little poodle led us down a winding path, with Mrs. B. lagging behind as she leaned on a walking cane. Without warning, Sprinkles stopped short of a twisted oak tree, her ears perked in full alert.

When I caught sight of Jughead arranging all the stolen trinkets into a heap, I knew we'd struck gold. He had an alarming amount of shiny objects stashed beneath the tree. As we approached, I looked up and noticed a few more items way up in the branches.

"Whoa!" Forest stepped up to the haul. "You're quite the scam artist, Jughead."

The tiny monkey huddled into a ball. He wasn't stupid. He knew he was in trouble.

Sadie finally caught up to us. "Look—here's Bert's fishing lure, and my brass teacup from my Aunt Ethel. Land sakes, he must've stolen stuff from everyone at the campground!" She shook her head.

Sprinkles began to bark at the little monkey. Her short leash kept jerking her back, preventing her from reaching her goal. She growled in frustration.

I was beginning to feel the same way.

We searched through the pile of rubbish and knick-knacks without any sign of the ring.

"Well, Sprinkles, we should get back to camp, but first you deserve a reward." Sadie reached in her pocket and pulled out a banana. "I know it's not your usual can of chopped liver, but it will have to do."

Removing the peel, she gave half to Sprinkles and handed the rest to Jughead before gathering her belongings and hobbling off with her poodle in tow.

The little monkey eagerly grabbed it and took a bite, revealing two rows of sharp serrated teeth.

"What if Grandpa's ring is up in the tree?" I said to Forest and Sailor, not wanting to give up hope. "If we could only reach those branches."

"We'd need a ladder for that." Forest used his hand to block the sun as he looked up into the tree.

Suddenly, a high-pitched rumble accelerating up the path caught our attention.

"Whoa, check it out." Forest motioned through a clearing to an enormous cylindrical ball made of metal.

There was a kid riding a dirt bike in circles inside it—even upside down. The rider stopped right in front of us as we approached and put the kickstand down.

Jughead dropped the banana and scrambled up a nearby birch tree.

"Dude, that was amazing! How did you do that?" Forest was obviously impressed.

"Not bad for a girl, huh?" She removed her helmet, tossing her long, black locks. "Hi, I'm Tessa. I know you guys. Your grandparents are getting engaged, right?"

I nodded, stunned, before narrowing my eyes at Sailor, who cowered under my glare.

"Hey—If you thought that was cool, I can do three in a row," Tessa offered. "Wanna see?"

"For sure!" Sailor chirped. "But first we need to find a ladder. Jughead stole a bunch of junk and some of it is up in this tree."

Tessa got back on the bike and revved the engine. "I think I know just the person who can help—wait here. It'll only take a minute," she said before doing a burnout and disappearing into a cloud of smoke.

"A girl with an attitude … I like that." Forest shoved his hands into his pockets.

"C'mon, stay focused." I nudged him. "Don't forget we have a mystery to solve."

"Geez, Dominic." He gave me the stink-eye. "Maybe some things should just remain a mystery."

It didn't take long until the answer to our prayers arrived: a tall young man walking on stilts, headed in our direction.

A little unconventional, but this should do nicely.

"Hey, over here, we could really use a hand," I called out to him.

"James the Gentle Giant at your service." The lanky boy on stilts steadily approached. He appeared to be very brave as he loomed overhead with great confidence. "Congratulations, by the way. I heard your grandparents are getting married. That's so cool!"

Sailor covered her eyes.

Ughhh. No use giving her a piece of my mind now. She knows she blew it.

"Thanks, but at this point, everything seems to be up in the air ... literally. See, up in the tree?" I pointed. "Jughead's been storing treasure on some of the branches. Do you think you can reach it?"

"I can give it a try." James took a few steps closer. "It's a little out of reach. Can you find something I can use to shake the branches?"

"Here, take this stick." I handed him a dead limb from off the ground.

It was just long enough to knock the trinkets out of the tree. Down came a keychain and an empty tube of lipstick. James rustled the limbs a little more, this time loosening a few leaves, when suddenly —

A small black box dropped to the ground right in front of us, landing with a thud.

CHAPTER 6

I grabbed the box and opened it, fully expecting to see GB's diamond ring inside and save the day.

It was empty. Dang! I showed Sailor and Forest.

"We'll never find GB's ring now." Sailor kicked the tree.

"She's right. Looking for a ring in the woods would be like spotting a needle in a haystack," Forest said.

"Sorry you didn't find what you were looking for." James shrugged. "I have to get back to practice. Archie's been acting out of sorts lately, and he'll be wondering where I've been."

"No problem." I forced a smile. "But when you said, 'out of sorts,' what exactly did you mean by that?"

"It's like he's going bonkers. I think it has something to do with an old girlfriend."

Could it be Windsong? My eyes widened.

"I guess you better go, then. Thanks for your help!"

James turned and lumbered back down the trail on his stilts.

"I wonder what James was implying about an old girlfriend?" I asked the others.

"All I know is it seems pretty irresponsible not to keep better track of your circus animals," Forest remarked. "Doesn't Archie have any idea what Jughead's been up to?"

"That's just it," I said. "Jug might be stealing off picnic tables, but how would he get into our camper? I know for a fact GB always keeps the door locked. I don't want to jump to conclusions, but someone must've put him up to it, and I'm betting that whoever it is kept the ring for themselves."

"We need to find out what Archie's up to." Forest dusted off his jeans.

"Good idea. I have a feeling that joker has a few tricks up his sleeve."

Embers smoldered from the campfire, and smoky spirals streaked through the trees like long fingers. The silence felt eerie without the typical hippie banter.

"Looks like we're in luck … no one's around, which means we can search for clues in Archie's tent." Forest had a wicked look in his eyes.

Sailor lowered her voice. "Okay, but Dominic should go first just in case someone's in there."

I gawked at her. "Why me?"

"To be our protector against angry clowns." Forest chuckled. "You've been working out … you said so yourself."

"Clowns have been getting a bad rap. You watch too much TV," I retorted.

We crept up alongside the candy-striped tent.

Forest pulled back the canvas flap that covered the doorway. The coast was clear, so I quietly slipped inside, followed by Sailor, while Forest stood guard.

A loud squawking sound got my attention. A red, yellow, and blue parrot in a cage was swinging back and forth. As I approached, his head bobbed back and forth as he unfurled his colorful wings.

My macaw, Pedro, does the same thing when he wants attention, so I knew the best way to keep the bird quiet was to ignore him, and it worked. After I turned my back and walked away, he settled down.

As I surveyed the tent searching for the best place to hide a ring, a handful of helium balloons caught my attention. They were tied to a makeup table, with a light-up mirror on top and a scattering of lipstick tubes, pencils, and powders on the counter.

Taped to the mirror was a picture of a lady with pink hair, swinging from a trapeze. The name "Lydia" was signed at the bottom.

Could this be the old girlfriend James mentioned?

Sailor began sifting through a large cedar storage

chest. I joined her as she pulled out a rubber nose and ears, but there didn't seem to be anything convicting Archie of a crime. It was all bowties, bouncy balls and juggling clubs.

Suddenly, Forest jumped up from where he stood at the door. "Someone's coming—hide!"

He flailed his arms at us before ducking behind an overstuffed armchair.

Sailor looked at me in a panic. Together we ran to the wardrobe stationed along the back wall and climbed inside. It was a tight squeeze among all the costumes.

I could feel my heart pounding in my chest. Neither of us dared to breathe.

"This will be the whipped topping on the banana cream pie!"

I recognized Archie's voice.

"A little over the top, don't you think?" a girl whispered.

"Desperate times call for desperate measures," he sneered.

"Alright, you're the boss."

I didn't recognize her voice, so I cracked open the door to see who it was. I had just caught a glimpse of a long swath of colorful fabric—almost like a cape, when Sailor started to sneeze.

She quickly pinched her nose, but it was too late.

"Did you hear something?" Archie's voice grew closer. A shadow loomed over the wardrobe as a hand reached toward the door.

My forehead beaded with sweat.

The parrot began rattling his cage, agitated.

"Peek-a-boo, peek-a-boo." *Squawk!*

"Never mind. It's only Houdini," Archie said as he turned to walk away.

I sighed with relief.

"This is going to be our best performance yet!" Archie gave a sinister laugh. "Bob Dorsey will never know what hit him."

CHAPTER 7

When Archie and the mystery girl finally left the tent, Sailor and I slipped out of the wardrobe and joined Forest, who had already high-tailed it out of there. The three of us ran for cover inside Windsong's trailer, shutting the door behind us.

"That was a close one!" Forest caught his breath.

"Yeah. Sailor almost gave us away."

"I couldn't help it." She scrunched up her face. "One of Archie's wigs kept tickling my nose."

"Hey—what's that nauseating smell?" I fanned the air. A smoky haze filtered through the psychedelic décor, filling the trailer with a sweet, musky fragrance.

"That's just Windsong's incense." Sailor pointed to a ceramic cat incense burner with a small pile of ashes at the bottom.

Forest cranked open a window. "Happy now?"

Without waiting for an answer, he collapsed onto

his bed and propped his head on the pillow. "Hey, could either of you make out who Archie was talking to?" he asked. "Her voice sounded familiar."

"No idea, but she was wearing a colorful cape," I recalled. "So, it had to be one of the circus performers. Maybe we should go over and check things out?"

The circus troupe was in full swing by the time we arrived on the grounds. Vendors tidied up their display booths while others helped carry in stage props. A brown-and-white paint horse was tied to a hitching post near the big tent.

"Hey guys, say hi to Zippy." Sailor walked over and rubbed the horse's muzzle.

I gave her a quick scratch behind the ears. Zippy seemed to like it because her tongue was hanging out of her mouth. I wondered if that was part of the act.

We made our way inside to find many students busy practicing their routines. Archie and the mystery girl, however, were nowhere in sight. *Go figure.*

We paused for a moment to watch a tightrope walker in a pink tutu pedal a unicycle backwards and forward on the rope while holding a frilly umbrella.

A tiny girl with curly hair called up to her from beneath the safety net. "Hey, Fashionista — you're looking pretty good up there. When you're finished can you come and spot me?"

"Sure, Bibby! I'll be right there." Fashionista made her way across the rope and onto a platform. After climbing down the ladder, she stationed herself on a mat next to a pair of uneven bars while Bibby began to ready herself at the other end.

"On the count of three." Fashionista nodded. "One, two, three…"

Bibby took a deep breath and sprinted forward, planting both feet on the springboard. The momentum jolted her high into the air where she completed a flip before grabbing the top bar and landing solidly.

"Nice work!" Sailor cheered as she walked backwards with her head still in the clouds, accidentally bumping into a girl dressed in a black, purple, and red outfit who was holding a match in one hand, kerosene in the other.

Upon the collision, fire abruptly came shooting out of the performer's mouth. Flames burst right in front of Sailor's face as she let out a high-pitched scream.

"Oh, butternut!" The girl apologized. "Did I scare you?"

"Uh—yeah!" Sailor rubbed her forehead. "But I'm okay. I think my eyebrows are only *slightly* singed!"

"Next time, we'll be sure to bring some marshmallows." Forest laughed.

"Sorry about that. I'm Olivia—the fire spitter. Are you three joining the circus?"

"No, we were looking for Archie. Do you know where we can find him?" I asked.

"Um, last I saw he was outside helping Savannah train her tiger. But watch out, she has a short temper and so does her friend, Lexi the knife thrower."

"Thanks for the heads-up." I nodded.

Leaving through the back exit we walked toward the animal trailers. Passing by bales of hay, feed bags, and buckets for water, we came across some of the more exotic pets traveling with the circus.

A blond-haired, blue-eyed girl was coaxing a black bear to stand on two legs. The bear only licked its paw, uninterested.

"Let's go—hup!" She lifted her arms in an upward motion, but the bear rolled over instead.

"Nice work, Goldilocks!" Forest called over his shoulder.

The bear trainer giggled. "It's Brooklyn."

Sailor looked like she wanted to run over and give the bear a hug, but I kept my distance. After last summer's run-in with a bear, I knew not to mess around.

"There they are." Forest pointed to a roped-off

area nestled between two trailers.

Archie was watching a tall girl with a blue side ponytail dressed in a red trainer's jacket work with her tiger. The magnificent striped cat instinctively followed her lead, jumping from one platform to another.

"Great work, Savannah. Now try the hoop."

She held it up between the platforms and gave a command. This time, the tiger leaped through the hoop to the other side.

"Excellent! That's enough for today. Cloud will be ready for the show once I teach him the gate-opening trick."

"You want to train a tiger to open a gate? Are you sure about that?" Savannah shook her head and turned to pick up her red cowboy hat and trainer's whip.

"Lexi ... got a minute?" Archie called to a girl with rainbow-colored hair parted in two buns, wearing a white shirt and black pants with suspenders.

The girl looked up. I was hypnotized by her pale blue eyes. When she saw us watching, her face flushed.

"Be right there!" She set down the pair of knives she was sharpening and ran over to help Savannah lead Cloud back to his pen. I saw them whisper to each other as they both turned their heads in unison toward me.

I gave an awkward wave in their direction.

"Hey, kids!" Archie approached the three of us. "Can I help you?"

"As a matter of fact ..." I was ready to let him have it, when a low rumble muted my voice.

Ranger Rick drove his truck right through the yard. Somehow, he always managed to show up at the worst possible moment.

"Great—here comes the general," Archie grumbled. "Don't do this, you can't do that. Yada, yada. He even pulled me over in my clown car!"

Ranger Rick stormed toward Archie. "There's been a complaint that your primate's been caught red-handed—stealing, in laymen's terms. I expect everything to be returned to the rightful owners, or there'll be a hefty fine to pay."

The ranger eyed the circus grounds with a piercing glare. "And look at this place! Bears and tigers roaming about, guns going off, knives flying through the air, galloping horses—it's mass hysteria!"

"You're entitled to your opinion, but I'm not going to agree with you, or we'd both be wrong," Archie said.

Ranger Rick looked as though he was reaching boiling point until the sound of static distracted him.

Kwitch … "Ranger, do you copy …"

Ranger Rick grabbed his walkie-talkie from the holster on his belt. "Go ahead, Ranger Sally."

"We have an Evel Knievel coming through, doing a high-speed stunt on a motorcycle. Should be in your back pocket any moment." *Kwitch* …

"10-4." Without another word, he raced to the truck, shifting in reverse before speeding off.

Archie cupped his hands around his mouth and leaned into me. "There goes Officer Wackadoo. Am I right?"

"No, the ranger's right!" *I can't believe those words*

actually came out of my mouth. "Jug's been stealing stuff."

"Whoa, there … no need to get excited." Archie raised his hands.

Instead of explaining, he directed us toward the aroma of popcorn and mini donuts coming from the concession cart. "Why don't we discuss this over lunch?"

"Sounds good to me, Uncle Jolly," Sailor said.

"Uncle what-now?" Archie's eyebrows rose.

"Emily said all the kids call you that," Sailor insisted.

"Not all the kids. Just Emily. I'm her uncle." Archie glanced at his cell phone. "Let me clean up, and I'll meet you there in a minute."

He hurried off.

"Did you guys hear that?" I scratched my head. "Why would Emily lie to us about Archie being her real uncle?"

"I don't know. They don't even talk the same," Sailor noted. "Emily is so much more … proper."

My thoughts wandered as we headed toward the concession stand, identified as "JODY'S FOOD CART" across the top.

A freckled, blonde-haired girl stood ahead of us at the window, placing her order.

"Hey, it's May, the trick rider!" Sailor said.

"That would be me." May scooped a handful of popcorn from the red and white cardboard box in her hand. "Congrats on the upcoming wedding in your family! I once rented out Zippy for a wedding. She carried the rings on a pillow strapped to her saddle."

"Cool!" I said. "I can ask Grandpa Bob if he's interested in something like that."

"Yeah, or maybe Jughead could carry the ring!" Sailor chimed in.

"You mean the same monkey who ran off with it in the first place?" Forest snickered. "Wait a minute ..."

He stared at a young woman who was scrolling on her phone nearby. "I think I see the illusionist who's part of the monkey act with Archie and Ginny!"

She was wearing a multi-colored cape.

CHAPTER 8

We stepped up to Jody's Food Cart to order. A middle-aged woman with a kind face leaned out the window.

"Hi, kids! Welcome to my concession stand. What will it be?"

Sailor began hemming and hawing over what flavor snow cone to get.

"Let's see—we have raspberry-lemonade, cherry, grape …" Jody read off the display.

"Hurry up, Sailor. We gotta go!" I didn't want to let the rainbow caper out of our sight. Carla might be our ticket to finding GB's missing ring.

"Where's the fire?" Jody dropped a basket of do-nuts into the deep fryer and nodded at me. "How about you boys order first while she decides?"

Forest asked for licorice, while I grabbed a Snick-ers from the candy bar assortment on the counter and felt in my pockets for some cash. They were empty.

"Um, I don't have any money. We thought Archie was going to pay for it."

"Don't worry." Jody smiled at me. "It's on the house. Archie treats his helpers very well."

"In that case, can I get a little of each flavor?" Sailor's eyes lit up like a Christmas tree.

Jody laughed, handing the triple-decker cone to her. "Good luck with that!"

"Guys, she's getting away!" I tossed my crumpled candy wrapper into the garbage as I scarfed down the last bite. We hurried to catch up with Carla as she made her way over to a nearby parked car.

"Hi, Carla!" Forest brushed his bangs from his eyes as we approached her. "Nice cape."

"Yeah. Are you going to do a magic trick with pies?" Sailor bit into her snow cone. "Ouch—brain freeze." She rubbed her temple.

"Why don't *you* do a magic trick and make yourself disappear?" Forest glared at her.

"How did you know about the pies?" Carla's eyebrows raised. "I was just headed for Christina's

Cakery in Two Rivers. Archie asked me to pick up a few pies for the show."

"Actually, where *is* Archie? We were supposed to meet him here," I said.

"You just missed him. I think he was making plans with Windsong for a party they're throwing at the group site tonight." She removed her sunglasses, revealing dark-brown eyes that matched her hair. "What did you need him for? Maybe I can help."

"We're looking into a theft report. A few things went missing around here." I locked eyes with her.

"Oh, yeah. You must be Dominic. I heard about your grandpa's ring. Are you sure it wasn't Jughead? I think he stole my lockpick. He's a trained pickpocket," she said. "Everyone knows that."

"Could be. Either that or someone planted a banana peel at the scene to throw us off their scent."

"I'll be sure to keep my eyes 'peeled' for you." Carla made air quotes with her fingers. "Well, I better get going. See ya later." She removed her cape, got behind the wheel, and took off.

We sat huddled in our fort which I'd built a few years back, but vandals and weather had taken their toll. Now it was nothing more than a few pieces of driftwood hovering over a bank of rocks and sand.

Forest passed around a bag of red and black licorice sticks. I have to confess, I'm a black licorice guy. I know that's against popular opinion.

"Let's put this puzzle together." I picked up a lone piece of driftwood that was lying in the sand, using it to point for added effect.

"We already established that Archie has an alibi, and there's no way he stole useless objects from all the campers. But the question is, did he train Jughead to be a thief to do his dirty work?"

"Yeah," Forest agreed. "And if so, did Jug leave his trademark, or did someone else leave the banana peel next to Nimrod to implicate him?"

"Exactly," I continued. "That leads to the question, did someone deliberately set up Jug to take the blame and cover their tracks?"

"It's obvious that Archie wants Windsong for himself. So, it's highly probable that he would try to sabotage GB and Windsong's relationship."

Drawing bullet points in the sand, I presented the evidence:

1: GB's ring is stolen.

2: A banana peel is left at the scene.

3: Other campers notice stolen items.

4: Archie has a half-baked scheme involving pies.

5: A clown hid by a tree with a bag of tomatoes.

"I assume the plan was to throw them at someone, but at the sight of Ranger Rick they fled the scene."

"What are you getting at, Dominic?" Forest reached for a red licorice stick.

"Just this. We know that Archie has it in for GB, and this clown just happens to be hanging around the trail with a bag of tomatoes right when GB is about to walk through. Coincidence? I think not."

"That makes sense." Forest chewed thoughtfully. "But since Archie was at the hippie site, he must've coerced someone else into doing his dirty work."

"Sailor," I pointed the stick in her direction, "you mentioned Ginny was at your campsite last night. What time did she get there?"

Sailor rubbed her chin. "I'm sure I didn't see her until after Archie and the illusionist did their magic."

"Which means Ginny could've been on the scene," I said, growing excited, "*and* since she's a clown in training, she must have a clown costume somewhere."

Forest raised his hand. "What about Carla? Couldn't she be the ring thief?"

"That would be hard to do if someone stole your lockpick."

"Nothing personal, Dominic, but have you looked at Nimrod lately?" Forest pointed out. "It's held together by a thread. If someone wanted to get in there, I'm sure they could take out a window or something."

"Thanks for the reminder, Forest. I realize GB's camper is less than ironclad, but regardless ..."

"Not to mention, we saw Carla wearing a cape, just like the accomplice from Archie's tent," Forest added.

"Right, we definitely need to keep her on our radar." I thought for a moment. "Do we have any other suspects besides Ginny and Carla?"

"It could be anyone. Thanks to Sailor's big mouth, we lost any advantage we had on the circus performers."

Forest threw a small stone at Sailor's head. Sailor saw it coming and ducked out of the way.

"So what we can gather is that Archie is the ringleader using his lackeys to do his bidding." I plugged along. "Here's what we need to consider: is there anyone else among the circus crew he might confide in?"

"What about Emily? They're related," Sailor said. "If anyone would have dirt on Archie, chances are it would be someone close, like a family member."

As far as I was concerned, she'd just redeemed herself. "True! I definitely agree that there could be more to 'Uncle Jolly' than meets the eye."

"Sounds like we have our next move," Forest said.

"Right," I agreed. "We need to stop that clown before he puts his plans into motion. The future of our grandparents depends on it."

CHAPTER 9

Heading back to the group site was the logical place to continue the investigation. The hippies were throwing a party and invited the performers, which meant everyone would be conveniently gathered in the same place.

The campsite was lit up with torches and colored hanging lanterns. 70's music played from a boom box on a picnic table. It looked like the festivities were well underway.

I pulled Forest and Sailor aside. "This might be our last chance to look for clues. Consider everyone a suspect. We need to know if Archie took the ring or if one of his sidekicks is helping him."

We decided to split up and mingle.

I found GB hunched over the grill, mindlessly poking the coals with tongs. He was worse than expected, and I wasn't about to make it any better.

"Hey, Grandpa Bob. I hate to be the bearer of bad news, but we found the ring box. It was empty."

GB sighed and closed the lid. "I already know — the monkey took it."

"Don't get too down in the dumps. We still have a few theories to work out, but in the meantime, you might want to consider using the mood ring or coming up with plan B. Where is Windsong, anyway?"

"She's busy setting up for the party. I'm surprised she's not with Archie," he grumbled. "They've only been together practically all weekend."

"Hey, mister." Windsong walked over with a box of ginger snaps tucked under her arm. "Isn't this going to be a groovy party?"

GB brightened at her arrival with a big smile on his face — until Archie came up behind her. "It *was* …"

"Windsong," Archie grabbed her shoulder, "I need to talk to you."

"Sure thing." She turned to face him.

GB gathered his cooking utensils in a fluster. "I hate to interrupt your important conversation, but is the tofu ready? I've got the grill fired up."

"Are you serious? Everyone knows you don't make tofu on the grill." Archie laughed at GB, then turned back toward Windsong. "Wow, he *is* an old-timer!"

"Takes one to know one." GB's temper sparked. "Well, it was nice talking to you, Archie, but Windsong and I are busy over here."

"Doesn't look that way to me, and I don't like your tone. Do we need to settle this man to man?"

"You mean *clown* to man," GB retaliated.

Windsong planted herself between them. "Archie, you're sounding like a childish schoolboy. I'm surprised at you," she scolded.

"How come you're not surprised by me?" GB flipped up his palms.

Windsong laughed. "You boys are hilarious. I'd love to join in, but I have to help get the hors d'oeuvres ready."

I wanted to ask Archie why he ditched us at the concession stand, but now was obviously not the time.

help can be a handful."

"Hey, guys, are you 'diggin' the party?" Bibby joined us with a can of Orange Crush in her hand.

A girl after my own heart.

Suddenly I felt a little thirsty myself. "I'm going to get a drink. Do any of you ladies want anything?" I nearly fell backward while trying to get off the bench.

The girls giggled as I excused myself.

Perfect timing—I spotted Emily sitting by herself at the fire. Just the person I wanted to talk to. I grabbed a soda out of the cooler and headed her way.

"So, how'd you end up joining a circus?" I asked as I sat next to her.

My plan was to initiate some small talk while dangling a carrot in front of her to see if she would finally admit the truth that Archie was her *real* uncle.

Emily hesitated. "It's a long story."

"Well, it just so happens I love long stories." I popped open my soda.

"Here goes, then," she said, kicking off her flipflops. "The circus, you might say, runs in my blood.

My parents were trapeze artists, my cousins were stunt performers, and my grandparents worked in one of those 'freak show' carnivals. You know — the kind with peculiar people?" She grinned at me. "A bearded lady, a mermaid, a dog-faced man, etc. They traveled like gypsies, living out of their trailers like vagabonds."

"Sounds like some hippies I know." I took a swig of soda.

Emily stared into the flames. "Aye, but it got old. Everything does, when a bloke has to work for his bread and butter. It's a curiosity, innit?" The logs in the fire-pit continued sizzling with orange streaks of fire leaping and jumping.

"Do you think that's what happened to Archie — I mean — *Uncle Jolly*?" I narrowed my eyes. "Some of the other performers are talking like he flipped his lid. At least that's the vibe I'm getting."

"I'm completely embarrassed," Emily lowered her head, "but I really should confess ..."

Wait for it ... Wait for it ...

"Never mind. It's just poppycock," she said.

Her slang was throwing me for a loop. I decided to take a different approach.

"Well, something's been bothering me for a while now, but maybe you can shed some light on it," I said. "There's a picture on Archie's dressing table—a lady flying on a trapeze with neon pink hair."

"Oh, that's Lydia," she confirmed. "Archie's had his knickers in a twist ever since she left him for some other clown."

Emily was about to say more when a commotion from inside Archie's tent interrupted our conversation, right when I was about to get the scoop on Lydia.

CHAPTER 10

"Get your butt back here, you ungrateful mongrel!" Archie stormed out of his tent, shaking his fist at Jughead.

Jug ran past us, a tiny white box with green lettering in his hands.

"Fiddlesticks. He's at it again." Emily pulled a whistle from her pocket and blew it. The shrill high-pitched sound stopped Jughead in his tracks long enough for her to take the box from him.

She looked at the label before tossing it back to Archie. He caught it with a grunt and disappeared back into the tent.

"What's in the box?" I asked.

"Green food coloring. Who knows what that clown is up to?" Emily shrugged.

A light breeze swept through the trees, cooling the night air. The sky had grown dark and things were beginning to die down at the hippie campsite.

Emily yawned. "Tomorrow's a big day. Best get some shuteye."

"Goodnight, then. And good luck on the show tomorrow!"

"Okay. Tickety-boo." She turned and headed toward a row of pup tents in the woods.

No idea what that even means.

I saw Forest nearby, deep in conversation with Tessa the dirt biker. I started heading his way and caught his eye, motioning for him to join me. I was hoping he had learned something at tonight's party. Time was of the essence.

"There you are." I grabbed him by the elbow and pulled him aside. "Were you able to come up with anything? We do have a mystery to solve, you know."

"Geez, Dominic." He shook free of my grasp and motioned toward Tessa. "We were just making plans to go dirt biking."

I gave him the deadpan stare—the kind actors use to intimidate people in thriller movies where you look annoyed and demanding all at once.

"Okay, okay!" Forest followed me behind a nearby tree. "I did have a, uh … a revelation."

He must've noticed the stupid smile on my face.

"So, I had this idea …" He nervously looked to his left and right before looking back at me. "It's just a hunch, really."

"Try me."

Forest looked at the ground. "Ehh, so the thing is … the thing is … you know, like, how a person puts up a camera when thieves start stealing Amazon packages from their porch?"

"Um. Yeah, I know about that." I scratched my head.

"Okay," he said. "So, I did that before — three or four times … or two." He looked at the ground. "Maybe just once."

"You're killing me, Forest!" I exclaimed. "What, exactly are we talking about here?"

"I may have taken down one of Ranger Rick's trail cams that he put up after last year's bear scare and set it outside Archie's tent."

I started laughing. "You set up a camera? I don't know if that's a crime, but I doubt it will help anything, though. The circus is taking place tomorrow, and after that they're all leaving."

"I set it up two days ago."

"So how come I'm just now hearing about this?"

Forest looked at his feet. "Sorry, Dominic. You seem so, like, old-school. I didn't think you'd approve."

"Well, it is what it is. Have you watched the footage yet?" I leaned around the tree and glanced at the group of people sitting around the fire pit to make sure no one was listening in.

Nothing to worry about there; they were all laughing at Jughead's antics. He was doing tricks for the shelled peanuts Harmony was throwing to him.

"Yep, I popped in at the trailer after we got here." He combed his hand through his hair. "I guess you could say we're movie stars. Picture it—three kids break into a guy's tent and almost get caught."

"Whoa! Not good." I got quiet for a few minutes. "Did you see anything else, or … anyone else?"

"As a matter of fact," he cleared his throat, "I noticed one person who visited Archie quite frequently. A certain individual in a cape."

"And? Was it Carla, as we suspected?"

"Nope. It was Ginny. She carried a paper bag out of the tent. Same kind of bag the tomatoes were in." Forest leaned against a tree and crossed his arms. "If it wasn't for setting up that camera, we'd have never known what a sneak Ginny is."

"Guys, guys! I was looking all over for you." Sailor ran up, stopping to bend over and catch her breath. "I have breaking news!"

I perked up. "That's awesome. What is it?"

"Okay, so I went for a slushie at the food cart. I talked to Jody." She had a knowing look on her face, as if that information alone would send us to the moon. "Well, I asked Jody about Emily. Like, how did she end up here all the way from England?"

We continued to stare at her.

She took a deep breath before continuing. "It turns out, Emily ran away from home!"

Forest and I looked at each other.

"Yeah, she came here to join the circus!"

I rubbed my chin. "Well, that is *very* interesting. You know, Emily was starting to tell me a secret before. Maybe that was it," I said. "I guess if Archie is really her uncle, it makes sense that she would join him here, but there's something else I almost forgot about."

"Let's hope it's good," Forest quibbled. "Sailor and I can't do all the work around here."

"Oh, it is. Emily told me Archie's hung up on a lady with pink hair named Lydia. Not to mention, Ginny made a comment that Archie had a surprise planned for Windsong. Something's up—we just have to make the connection."

"Ah, Dominic, I think we have a situation." Forest lowered his voice to a whisper.

I followed his stare over to Ranger Rick bending down to examine the trail cam set up near Archie's tent. He spun around just as the three of us were sneaking out from behind the shadow of the tree.

"Hold it there, buck-o."

We froze.

"On a scale of one to ten … how mad do you think he is right now?" I whispered, glancing back.

"I'd say a fourteen," Sailor guessed. "Did we do something wrong?"

"We'll see." I prepared for the worst, but to my surprise, Ranger Rick didn't seem to notice us.

Instead, he headed straight for Archie, who was bringing Jughead into his tent for the night.

"Stop right there, Mr. Valentine. We never got to finish that talk about your pickpocket pet." Ranger Rick approached him with the camera in hand. "Perhaps you'd like to explain how *this* ended up outside your premises?"

"Must you question everything I do?" Archie scowled.

"Everything you do is questionable." Ranger Rick tapped his foot.

"If you think I stole it—then you're barking up

the wrong tree — end of discussion, my friend."

"Either you, or that monkey who you 're supposedly in charge of."

Jug stuck out his tongue and made a spitting sound. Ranger Rick took off his hat and shooed him away.

Archie glanced down at his wrist at an imaginary watch. "My, how time flies. As you know, I have a busy schedule tomorrow and you shouldn't leave your lady friend waiting."

He nodded toward Sally who sat in the passenger seat of the ranger's truck with a sour look on her face, her head propped up by her hand.

"Once I review these pictures, you won't be able to walk away so easily," Ranger Rick warned. "I'll see you tomorrow."

"Come early if you want good seats ..." Archie called after him before turning in for the night.

My eyes bugged out. *There's evidence of our break-in on that camera! If Ranger Rick uses it against us, we could be headed for juvie detention.*

CHAPTER 11

♫   *DOOT-DOOT-da-da-da-da-DOOT-DOOT-da-da-DOOT-DOOT-da-da-da-da-DOOT-DOOT-da-da* ♪

The fast-tempo circus music blared from the surround-sound system as we entered the big red-and-white-striped tent. Brightly colored lights and thundering brass horns filled the air as we searched for available seats.

Windsong was passing out cotton candy in the stands when she noticed us coming down the center aisle. "Over here! We saved seats for you."

She lifted the strap over her head that held a box of pink and blue confectionary sugar spun onto sticks, handing it to one of the other workers.

We had just settled in next to GB when the music stopped, and a hush settled over the crowd.

I leaned toward Forest. "I'm worried about the footage on that camera. The three of us could be in big trouble if we get caught for breaking and entering."

"Chillax, Dominic. I got you covered. The entire episode was erased."

A wave of relief washed over me.

Sailor was smacking on bubblegum and started blowing a huge bubble—it got bigger and bigger until Forest reached over and popped it with the tip of a pretzel stick, resulting in a loud pop that pierced the silence.

She jabbed Forest in the ribs.

"Hey, the show's starting," I whispered to them.

"Ladies and gentlemen, boys and girls, step right up," a voice boomed throughout the tent. "Welcome to the greatest show on Earth!"

Archie's face was painted white with a black diamond drawn above each eye. His lips were a darker red than usual. He stood at center stage in a long-tailed coat and a jester hat covering his curly red hair, with Jughead perched on his shoulder.

"With us tonight are some of the most talented young people I've ever seen, all the way from New

York to give you one heck of a show!" he announced.

The audience applauded. Lights flashed around the canvas walls in every direction.

The Buckley's sat in the row ahead of us. Bert's head drooped and a rattling wheeze escaped his lips as he started snoring loudly.

Sadie hit him over the head with her cane. That did the trick. He jolted awake.

To start the show, Archie announced each performer as they began to parade across the stage from one end to the other.

First came Lexi the knife thrower, followed by Bobert the sharpshooter, and Olivia the fire-spitter. Then Fashionista the tightrope walker and Bibby the gymnast flipped across the stage, each wearing sparkling singlets with frills on the sleeves.

Brooklyn the bear trainer marched out with Cory the human cannonball, Savannah the animal tamer, Arnissella the juggler, Ginny the clown, and James on stilts. Then Carla the illusionist appeared in a cloud of smoke, twirling her colorful cape before the audience.

Strobe lights raced across the stage as the back door opened to let May the trick rider enter on Zippy while standing up in the saddle, along with Tessa doing a wheelie on her dirt bike.

The audience went wild; people whistled, hooted, and hollered as the performers went by.

"Last, but not least, let's get the ball rolling with Emily, my ringmaster understudy," Archie said, stepping aside as Emily walked on stage wearing a black long-tailed coat, top hat, and knee-high boots, holding a whip in her hand.

She curtsied, then waved to the left and right sides of the stage to dismiss the performers, except one. "I give you Arnissella—she can juggle your apples and oranges 'til you don't know the difference. Just watch this!"

A girl in black polka-dot pants, a pink T-shirt, white vest and tiny white hat began juggling fire torches—three torches, then four, then five.

As I stared, I noticed she had a pink heart on her cheek—*nice touch.*

After she successfully juggled the torches, she took a bow and exited the stage.

"Alright, ladies and gents," Emily continued, "for our next act, please give it up for Bobert the sharp-shooter!"

The crowd went wild as a tall young man with a bolt-action rifle ran up on the stage. When he tipped his cowboy hat, his brown hair reflected red in the circus lighting.

I glanced at Sailor, pretty sure she would be swept off her feet by this gallant knight. Sure enough, her eyes had stars in them.

"Can I get a volunteer?" Bobert scanned the seats.

Forest stuck two fingers in his mouth and wolf-whistled, pointing to Sailor. She didn't wait for an invitation. She ran up to the stage like the next contestant on *The Price is Right*, nearly knocking Bobert over.

"Whoa, settle down there, chief." He grinned, revealing a space between his two front teeth.

Bobert positioned Sailor in front of a target.

"Now hold still, young lady. This won't hurt a bit," he said, placing an apple on her head. He slowly began to walk backward, with his rifle in hand.

The audience gasped.

Sailor must've thought she was the target. "No!" she screamed. The apple fell to the floor with a thump, and she ran back to her seat.

Bobert dismissed her with a wave, and aiming his rifle at the *real* target, he shot a hole in the middle of the bullseye.

Now that's what I call a show.

Next up, Archie came on stage wearing a ranger's suit with an oversized hat on his head and a gold star pinned to his shirt. He was spying on the circus performers through large binoculars and handing them violation tickets.

He shook a white-gloved finger at Bibby for jumping rope and handed her a ticket. Lexi threw a knife at a target—she got a ticket, too—and he even gave Zippy the horse a ticket. But when Brooklyn walked by with her bear, he ran off.

Ranger Rick sat next to Sally in front row seats. I don't think he appreciated the joke at his expense.

As he turned back and scowled at the audience, I noticed his eyes were going in circles like a pinwheel, his ears bright red.

The crowd kept laughing. Sally laughed so hard that tears started rolling down her cheeks.

Many more young stars amazed the audience by their gravity defiance, balancing acts, and contortion abilities, but I was particularly waiting for Carla's illusion tricks, and Ginny the clown's fortune telling act.

I hoped to glean more about the circus "suspects," but Archie was probably saving that for the end.

"We will now take a short intermission," Emily announced. "In the meantime, here's Ginny the clown with her parrot, Houdini, to entertain you with a little open mic improv."

Ginny took the stage wearing a colorful cape just like Carla's, with Houdini on her shoulder. She looked mysterious in her jeweled turban. Her eyes were lost in blue eye shadow, and her lips were painted black.

"Is there anyone out there who'd like to come up and share their talent with us tonight?" She asked.

A girl who looked about 10-years-old who introduced herself as Brandy, stepped up with her ventriloquist dummy, Randy. She performed a short skit that was quite good for her age. Everyone laughed when they both drank water from a cup, and Randy's water dribbled down his wooden chin.

"Cool," I said to Sailor. "I want to be a ventriloquist so I can talk to a dummy!"

"You already are." Forest snorted, trying to hold back the laughter.

After Brandy took a bow, she headed back to her seat and Ginny came forward again. "Anyone else? We have a few more minutes for open mic. Step right up!"

Houdini whistled and shrieked, "Toss the pie, toss the pie!" *Squawk* …

Hmmm. The parrot got me thinking – was he repeating something he heard? But a rhythmic *tap, tap, tap* pulled me out of my thoughts.

"Is this thing on?" a familiar voice asked.

The audience chuckled at the strange old man tapping away at the microphone.

Who let Mr. Buckley up there? I cringed.

"Since there's a little interlude, how 'bout I tell a joke?" Bert stood up to the microphone stand.

"Two silkworms entered a race ..." He slapped his knee while letting out a bellow of laughter. "They ended up in a tie."

He went on like that for some time. Kind of embarrassing.

Sadie sighed. "His jokes are about as funny as a flat tire." She motioned for him to get off the stage, but he ignored her.

"My wife keeps bananas in her pocket, because her doctor said she's low on potassium. Well ... my doctor told me to start eating more potato chips, because at my age, I need all the preservatives I can get!"

Finally, the crowd gave a chuckle.

Archie stepped in and took the mic. "What a natural! Well, you know what they say: 'He who laughs last ... thinks slowest.'"

He swung the microphone around by its cord before grabbing it in his other hand like a yoyo.

"Alright folks, it's been a delight here at Point Beach. We hope you were entertained this evening!"

The crowd cheered and whistles sounded in the big tent as the night was coming to an end.

"Did you know there've been quite a few world records set in Wisconsin?" Archie continued. "The tallest toilet paper pyramid, the largest collection of Smurf memorabilia, and the most touchdown passes at Lambeau Field ... but what impressed me was the man who ate 28,788 Big Macs—not to mention the one who drank a liter of gravy. What's wrong with you people?"

I could hear the crowd groan from all around me as my own stomach did a few flips.

"Now, we will attempt a small feat of our own." Archie stepped aside.

Two stagehands carried in a long table covered with a white sheet, setting it in the center of the ring.

Archie pulled back the sheet, revealing a dozen cream pies. "I'm going to need a volunteer." He scanned the seats, pin-pointing GB. "How about you, kind sir?"

A spotlight shined on GB's bald head.

"Go on, Bobby." Windsong gave him a nudge.

GB folded his arms across his chest. "Over my dead body."

"Careful what you wish for," Forest muttered.

"I guess I'll have to do it, then." Windsong was about to get up when GB turned, placing his hands on her shoulders. "Oh, no—if Archie wants to get to you, he's going to have to go through me, first."

"C'mon, man." Jim came over from a few seats behind and coaxed GB into the aisle. "Just go with the flow. This is gonna be outta sight!"

As he made his way to the stage, I suddenly re-called Archie's scheme regarding the whipped cream pies.

Grandpa Bob was walking right into a trap.

CHAPTER 12

Jughead jumped onto the table, dressed in a tiny circus coat and top hat held by a band under his chin. He stuck his paw in a pie and licked the cream from his fingers.

Arnissella the juggler snuck up behind the table and gently shoved him off.

I turned to Forest. "Stay on high alert. I think Archie's up to something."

He gave me a thumbs up.

Archie ushered GB across the stage and placed him in front of the table. Arnissella held an oversized bib, ready to tie it around GB's neck.

"Who wants to see Bob Dorsey set a record in the World Pie-Eating Championship?"

The crowd cheered loudly.

GB looked like a deer caught in the headlights.

"No pressure—all you need to do is eat four pies

in less than three minutes." Archie had a crazed look in his eyes. He pounded the table with a fork clutched in his fist.

The crowd seemed entranced, chanting, *"Eat the pie! Eat the pie!"* All I could do was nervously wait for the charade to unfold.

"Not going to happen." GB didn't flinch.

"Very well—you asked for it ..." Archie shrugged. "Here comes the consolation prize."

I noticed movement from behind the curtain.

"Grandpa, duck!" I yelled, just as Ginny stood poised with a pie in her hand.

GB heard me and dropped to the floor. The pie sailed right past him, landing smack-dab on Arnissella's head, covering her in green slime.

"Ewwww!" she cried, using her hands like windshield wipers to remove the green cream from her eyes.

"Now, folks. It's all part of the show." Archie quickly escorted Arnissella off the stage.

"I highly doubt that." I turned to Forest and Sailor. "We better go help GB."

We got up and hurried to the stage along with Windsong, just as Emily announced there'd be another short intermission.

GB stood off to the side looking like he was about to blow his steam as he brushed himself off. "What kind of a three-ring circus is this? That's what I'd like to know."

"Now, Bobby. It's just good fun," Windsong said. "I'm sure Archie didn't mean any harm."

"No harm? That green slime pie was meant for me. He's had it in for me ever since we got here."

The curtain parted and Archie reappeared on stage driving a clown car and tooting an air horn. He stopped short in front of Windsong. The sight of GB holding her hand only seemed to escalate his delirium.

"You wouldn't know the meaning of romance if it hit you between the eyes!" Archie scoffed at GB as he stepped out of the car and returned to the stage front to address the audience. His voice rang loudly through the microphone, "And now, for the grand finale, may I have a married lady stand up, please?"

Ranger Sally hung her head in disappointment. Several ladies stood, but Mrs. Buckley was the closest. Archie pulled her up onto the stage. "Madame, if you would so kindly lend me your wedding band."

Sadie was quick to oblige. She began to yank on her ring, but it wouldn't budge.

Archie grabbed hold of the ring and began to tug on it until it finally slipped off her finger. "Too many bananas, Madame."

Everyone laughed.

"Voila!" Archie held up the ring to the audience. "For your inspection, we have a gold wedding band. It looks to be engraved." He read the inscription, "Forever yours, Teddy Bear."

That brought up a few titters from the crowd.

Sadie's face flushed. "No, no. That's not what it says," she scolded.

Archie looked again. "My apologies. It reads, 'Forever yours, Bert.' How sweet."

"Yes, yes. That's it." She nervously laughed as

she tousled her blue curls.

"Now that we have that settled, let the magic begin!" Archie announced.

Carla appeared from behind the curtain, dressed in purple tights, a colorful cape and a furry pink plume on her headpiece that waved back and forth as she walked. She took the ring from Archie and called for her assistant.

Ginny came forward with a black box, holding it open and shaking it upside down for the audience to see that it was empty as she walked along the edge of the ring curb. She brought the box to Carla.

Carla placed the ring inside, closing the lid.

"Kazamm!" The illusionist waved her hand before lifting the lid, tipping the box toward the audience so they could see the ring had disappeared.

The people gasped. Sadie looked nervous.

"Never fear—it's all part of the act!" Archie walked forward and slammed the lid shut.

Carla waved her hand once more over the box and quickly opened the lid, releasing a puff of smoke.

"Ladies and gentlemen. I give you … the ring!"

Archie reached inside, pulling a silver band from the box. It had a small diamond set between two engraved hearts.

How did GB's engagement ring end up there?

"That's not my ring!" Sadie sounded mortified. "What kind of stunt are you trying to pull?"

Instantaneously, circus music played at a fast tempo; the stage lights settling in on Cory the human cannonball. The skinny kid in black climbed into the barrel of the cannon and was expelled into the air by a blast that echoed through the tent.

Streaming behind him was a white banner that read: WILL YOU MARRY ME?

"I can only imagine who that was meant for," Forest snidely remarked.

My jaw went slack.

When Cory hit the net in the shape of a bullseye on the other side of the tent, his suit turned red and white, and confetti floated down from the ceiling onto the main floor.

The circus performers gathered and cheered as the crowd hooted and hollered with anticipation. All eyes were on Archie, now down on one knee before Windsong.

GB paled. He ran up on stage, catching Archie off guard. "That's my ring!" he shouted. "I bought it for Windsong. You stole it from my camper!"

Archie gasped as he zeroed in on Windsong. "Lydia, is this true? Have you given your heart to another?"

"Archie, it's me, Windsong." She seemed just as puzzled as anyone else. "Who's Lydia?"

This was getting weird. I looked around for backup and found Ranger Rick and Ranger Sally already heading our way.

Out of nowhere, Jughead lowered himself from an overhead light, knocking off Ranger Rick's hat, and then swinging onto Archie's back. The lights dimmed as the monkey grabbed the ring and scurried away toward a shadowy figure standing near the side curtain.

Archie jumped in the clown car.

"Stop that clown!" I yelled.

"Lydia, my love! The circus needs us!" he cried as the two rangers ran up alongside the getaway vehicle and lifted him out by the arms.

The crowd stood and cheered for an encore.

"The show's over, folks. You can all go home now," Ranger Rick announced. "Thanks for coming to the 'one and only' circus performance you will ever see at Point Beach—I can guarantee it!"

"What about my ring?" Sadie stood in shock as she watched Archie get hauled off stage.

Just then, Jughead tugged on her sweater pocket. She felt inside, removing her hand in triumph. "Heavens, that little Bug brought it back!" She placed the band on her finger. "But where did it come from?"

"I believe the ringmaster understudy might know," I said while I watched Jughead scamper on all fours back toward the curtain.

A shadowy figure emerged from between the folds of fabric.

There stood Emily.

CHAPTER 13

Emily held the black box used for the illusion trick and opened it toward GB, and he reached inside.

Finally, the moment we were all waiting for—Grandpa Bob's ring.

The circus performers huddled around to watch.

"There needs to be some explaining for all of this, but first I need to do something I should've done a long time ago." GB took the ring, and facing Windsong, went down on one knee.

"Windsong, will you marry me?"

"Oh, Bobby, of course I will!" Windsong fell into his arms. "But don't you think this whole circus grand finale was a little overboard?"

GB kissed her on the cheek.

"Well, how do you like that, bro?" Forest slapped me on the back. "Or should I say, cuzz?"

"You can call me plain old Dominic."

"Suit yourself." Forest glanced over at Sailor. "Hey, 'plain old Dominic,'" he pointed at her, "do you think she's laughing or crying?"

Sailor had a goofy smile plastered on her face and tears streaming down her cheeks.

Truthfully, I was feeling a little choked up, too, but no way would I let on.

Emily made her way through the crowd. "I'd like to be the first to extend my congratulations, and to apologize for the trouble I've caused."

"Well, thank you, sweetie." Windsong smiled. "But there's nothing to be sorry about."

"Actually, there is." Emily looked down. "When Uncle Archie went off the deep end after Lydia jilted him, I decided someone needed to step in and take over. So, when I heard that Dominic's grandpa was going to propose, I saw it as the perfect opportunity to steal the ring and blame it on my uncle."

"I don't understand." Windsong tilted her head. "How did you know about the ring?"

"The entire campground knew Grandpa Bob was

going to propose, except for you," Sailor explained.

"Yeah. I wonder why?" Forest muttered.

Sailor punched him in the arm.

"So, Emily used Carla's lockpick to break into Nimrod, steal the ring, and leave a banana peel behind to frame her uncle for the crime," I explained. "One way or another, with Archie out of the picture, Emily could become the new ringmaster of the circus."

"So, the monkey *didn't* steal it out of my camper?" GB smoothed over a few wispy gray hairs on his head. "And Archie isn't to blame, either?"

"The only thing Archie wanted to do was have me hit you with a few rotten tomatoes and turn your face green," Ginny confessed. "Sorry about that, Arnisella."

The juggler who had been hit in the face by the pie now had green hair and eyebrows. "It's okay. It'll wash out. Besides—it actually tastes pretty good." She wiped a glob of cream from her nose and licked it off her finger.

"That makes sense! Archie was hiding green

food coloring in his tent. But what I'm wondering is, why did you go along with his scheme?" I questioned Ginny.

She shrugged. "Ever since Archie took me in, he's been like a father to me. I feel indebted to him. Besides, I thought it was all harmless fun. How was I supposed to know the circus would turn into a … madhouse?"

"Archie helped all of us," Lexi agreed.

"So, if your uncle wasn't such a bad guy, why'd you turn on him, then?" Forest asked Emily.

She put her face in her hands.

"I always dreamed of circus life in America, so I ran away from home to be here. My parents would've demanded I go back, if it weren't for Uncle Archie offering to train me. I was afraid I'd be packing my bags if he went cuckoo and couldn't run the circus anymore. The only solution I could find was to take over as ringmaster."

"Two wrongs don't make a right, young lady." GB wagged a finger at her. "But you're still learning.

So, I tell you what—we'll let things slide, seeing how there's no harm done and all. I must say, this has turned out to be one strange mystery."

Cannonball Cory triumphantly entered the tent, the edges of his outfit now noticeably singed. "Looks like the show will go on! Ranger Sally dropped Archie in the dunk tank. I think he's back to *normal* again," he said with a wide grin.

"What's all the hubbub?" Bert stopped in front of everyone. "Is it time to tell more jokes? Have you heard the one about the silkworms in a race before?"

"Not now!" Sadie interrupted him. "Can't you see that Windsong has a diamond ring on her finger?" Then with a wink, she added, "And it just so happens that Bert is a retired minister … just in case anyone is interested."

It got quiet all of a sudden. We probably all wondered the same thing: Is this really happening?

Grandpa Bob and Windsong turned and looked at one another shyly.

Now *this* was magic.

"Friends, family and creatures of the forest, we celebrate the union of two happy campers: Bob Dorsey and …" Bert cleared his throat, "um … Windsong." He nervously glanced in her direction, straightening his bow tie.

"Dominic, aren't you excited? What a happy day!" I sat with Mom in the front row. GB had called to invite her as soon as the arrangements were made.

"My goodness, I had no idea I'd be attending Pop's wedding this weekend." A tear slid down her cheek as she grabbed a handkerchief from her purse.

"It's awesome you're here, Mom. Now you can see for yourself the place where we solved all the mysteries." I took in my surroundings, feeling proud about our experiences here the past few years. I have to say, I was impressed. Harmony, Ranger Sally and Sadie really outdid themselves with the decorations.

"Wow, this looks like a scene from a fairy tale!" Sailor spun around to admire the white lights hanging down from the trees, and the gazebo covered in pine branches. Rustic wooden benches were arranged in rows, with a bouquet of wildflowers and baby's breath decorating the wooden torches along the benches.

A path of cedar chips wound its way to where Windsong stood; her hair woven with a garland of small pink flowers. Her dress, a simple off-white gown with beaded fringe. Her feet were bare.

She was definitely in her element.

GB looked as regal as one could look, considering the time frame. He'd managed to scrounge up a pair of black Levi's and a white polo shirt. Sadie had stuck a pink wildflower in the buttonhole of his shirt pocket.

The sound of strumming broke my thoughts. Jim walked up to the front with his guitar strapped over his shoulder, decked out for the occasion.

His long stringy hair was pulled up into a bun;

his black-and-white paisley shirt that he usually wore hanging loose was tucked into his pants. He began to sing:

♫ On the road of life in our hippie caravan

Chillin' at Point Beach, toes in the sand

Wedding bells are ringing for Bob and Windsong

Love was in the air all along,

All along … ♫

While Jim continued to play chords on his six-string, another hippie joined in, playing the bongos. I stared off into space, thinking about all the ways our camping trips would be different now…

What will happen to Nimrod? Will we all camp on one site next year? Will GB survive on Windsong's cooking?

Forest elbowed me. I looked up the aisle. GB was slipping the ring on Windsong's finger. The diamond sparkled in the sunlight.

"By the power vested in me by God and man, I now pronounce you husband and wife." Bert nodded at GB. "You may kiss your bride."

Sorry ... I can't detail this next part. Romance sort of makes me sick. I had to look away.

Rice rained down as GB and Windsong walked down the aisle. Ranger Sally was crying, black streaks of mascara running down her face.

As Windsong turned to throw the bouquet, all the eligible bachelorettes tried to catch it: Sailor, Ranger Sally, Harmony and Mom.

The bouquet looked like it was headed for Sailor, but Ranger Sally jumped in front of her and managed to grab the flowers at the last minute.

Her victorious gaze landed on Ranger Rick. He turned as red as a tomato.

After the ceremony, we headed to the lodge for the reception, where a surprise awaited us. Nimrod was parked out front with a "Just Married" sign plastered to it, along with a string of tin cans tied to the bumper.

"I wonder who did this?" GB walked up to it, scratching his head.

"Surprise!" Archie jumped out from behind the

camper. He was dressed in street clothes, but with his wild red hair he still looked like a clown.

"Archie?" Windsong joined GB, along with the rest of us. "Did you do all this?"

"Guilty. After all the shenanigans I pulled, I wanted to make it up to you. I tried to do right by these kids, but when Lydia ran off with my best friend, I lost my way. I thought if I could just redeem myself ..."

"Oh, Archie!" Windsong hugged him. "You don't need to explain. In fact, we sort of put two and two together." She winked at GB. "What happens now?"

"The kids are on their way to New York. I'll catch up with them later. But first, I have some unfinished business to take care of."

GB shrunk back.

Ranger Rick started making his way to the front, pushing through the crowd.

"No worries, old man," Archie patted him on the shoulder. "I plan on dropping in on Lydia and Chuckles to wish them well. It will bring closure. I wish both of you well, too. Maybe I'll see you next year."

They shook hands. GB was a man of few words, but his heart was in the right place.

Archie scanned our small group, his eyes locking on mine. "I hope you'll consider my invitation to join the circus, Dominic!"

And with that, he stretched out his wand. Three doves magically appeared. As they flew out of sight, he hopped into his orange VW Bug. Fumes poured from the exhaust pipe as he drove out of the parking lot.

We stood and watched the trail of smoke curl over the treetops until he was gone. I was going to miss that crazy, red-haired clown. It would sure be quiet around here now.

Inside the lodge, another surprise was waiting. Gold balloons hung from the ceiling, and a fire blazed in the fieldstone fireplace. A caterer had set the table with a feast for the wedding party.

"Well, Dominic, another mystery solved," Forest said as we filled up our plates. "So, what now? After all that excitement, are you tempted to join the circus?"

"Nah. I wouldn't want to get too far away from Point Beach. Something tells me I'll be helping out here again, somehow. Besides, how would Ranger Rick get by without me?"

We reached the end of the table where my favorite part of the meal was set up—dessert. I was expecting to see a fancy wedding cake with a plastic bride and groom on top, but instead there were banana cream pies.

What else?

JUST
MARRIED
NIMROD

Debby lives in Maribel, Wisconsin. She's a member of Pens of Praise Christian writers' group and enjoys family gatherings, country life and the four seasons.

Kate lives in Branch, Wisconsin. She's a member of Pens of Praise Christian writers' group and a church accompanist. She enjoys spending time with her family.

Connect with us online at:

Facebook.com/MysteryatPointBeach

Facebook.com/TheTinCanSeries

Our thanks to Anne Bender and Sarah Grosskopf, our beta readers, and our editor, Ben Wolf.

A very special thanks to Jody Siahaan and her 5th grade class of '20 –'21 who created the colorful circus characters for the story.

Books in the Mystery at Point Beach Series:

Book 1: Sundae Wars

Book 2: Pirate's Booty

Book 3: Alien Invasion

Book 4: Bushwhacked

Book 5: The Ringmaster

Book 6: Haunted Hemlock

Books in The Tin Can Series:

Book 1: Mystery at Flamingo Bay